STARBRIGHT®

Dear Reader,

 The power of stories . . .

 A story has the power to lift our spirits, transport us to new places, and offer us meaningful lessons. *Once Upon a Fairy Tale* also offers the opportunity to give seriously ill children a special gift, the freedom to just be kids.

 As Chairman of the STARBRIGHT Foundation, I've had the opportunity to meet some extraordinary kids who have heroically faced some very difficult circumstances. Imagine being a child with a long-term serious medical condition and facing not only the physical challenges of the medical condition, but also the pain, isolation, fear, and anxiety that accompany such an illness.

 STARBRIGHT unites experts in pediatric healthcare with creative and technical leaders from the entertainment and technology communities, to create innovative projects and programs to empower these kids to fight their battles. STARBRIGHT works to provide them with tools to help them live richer and more fulfilling lives. Medical research has demonstrated numerous benefits for seriously ill children using STARBRIGHT's programs, including decreased feelings of pain and anxiety, improved coping, and a greater sense of responsibility for managing their illness.

 STARBRIGHT's programs are distributed free of charge to seriously and chronically ill children and teens across the nation. Your support helps us to continue and expand our efforts.

 On behalf of the STARBRIGHT Foundation, I'd like to personally thank you for purchasing *Once Upon a Fairy Tale*. Each of the extraordinary illustrators and celebrities have made this book possible by donating their time and talents to this project. Thanks to great generosity of spirit on the part of all our contributors, we've created something that we hope you and your family will enjoy, and that will raise funds to help STARBRIGHT serve the needs of seriously ill children and teens across the country.

With sincere appreciation and best wishes,

Steven Spielberg
Chairman, STARBRIGHT Foundation

Once Upon a Fairy Tale

Once Upon a Fairy Tale

Four Favorite Stories Retold by the Stars

Little Red Riding Hood

The Frog Prince

Goldilocks and the Three Bears

Rumplestiltskin

VIKING

VIKING

Published by the Penguin Group

Penguin Putnam Books for Young Readers, 345 Hudson Street, New York, New York 10014, U.S.A.

Penguin Books Ltd, 27 Wrights Lane, London W8 5TZ, England

Penguin Books Australia Ltd, Ringwood, Victoria, Australia

Penguin Books Canada Ltd, 10 Alcorn Avenue, Toronto, Ontario, Canada M4V 3B2

Penguin Books (N.Z.) Ltd, 182-190 Wairau Road, Auckland 10, New Zealand

Penguin Books Ltd, Registered Offices: Harmondsworth, Middlesex, England

First published in 2001 by Viking, a division of Penguin Putnam Books for Young Readers.

1   3   5   7   9   10   8   6   4   2

LIBRARY OF CONGRESS CATALOGING-IN-PUBLICATION DATA

Once upon a fairy tale : four favorite stories / retold by the stars.

p. cm.

Summary: Individual characters share their points of view on four familiar fairy tales,

providing a new way of looking at each. The accompanying CD consists of celebrities such as

Nicolas Cage and Glenn Close reading the stories.

ISBN 0-670-03500-9 (hardcover)

1. Fairy tales—United States. 2. Children's stories, American. [1. Fairy tales. 2. Short stories.]

PZ8 .O574 2001   [E]—dc21   2001002505

Printed and bound in Mexico

Barbra Streisand's appearance courtesy of Columbia Records

STARBRIGHT

STARBRIGHT would like to thank the following people whose generous time, support,
and talent made *Once Upon a Fairy Tale* possible:

Karen Kushell
Senior Producer and Editor

Kati Banyai	Regina Hayes
Tim Cloutier	Marvin Levy
Kristy Cox	Kristie Macosko
Denise Cronin	Kevin Marks
Jill Davis	Janet Pascal
Mariann Donato	Susan Ray
Catherine Frank	Gen. H. Norman Schwarzkopf
Gang, Tyre, Ramer & Brown	Ellen Goldsmith Vein
Tony Gardner	Doug Whiteman

Steven Spielberg, the chairman of the STARBRIGHT Foundation,
for his leadership and creative casting instincts;

Karen Kushell, for her creativity, her talents as a producer, and her tireless dedication
to the STARBRIGHT Foundation. Without her, this book would not exist;

Peter Samuelson, the founder of the STARBRIGHT Foundation,
for his energy, insight, and direction;

Storyopolis' Fonda Snyder and Dawn Heinrichs, for their
creative vision in shaping the project from its inception and nurturing its evolution;

and David Haspel, whose idea of creating a celebrity fairy tale
to benefit STARBRIGHT inspired this book.

André Mika
Audio CD Producer and Director

Bruce Greenspan
Chief Audio Engineer

Recorded on location at: VoiceBox Studios, Los Angeles, California;
The Warehouse Recording Studio, New York, New York; McHale Barone Studios, New York, New York;
NBC Studios, New York, New York; Air-Edel Studios, London, England;
Planet Grande Pictures, Malibu, California; Ron Rose Productions, Inc., Tampa, Florida

Field Engineers:
Dennis Contreras, David Kelly, Roger Tallman, Tim Leitner, Jeff Hixon, Joey Decker

Music composed by:
Dr. Willis Delony, Joey Decker, André Mika; Disk Productions, Baton Rouge, Louisiana

SPECIAL THANKS TO THE FOLLOWING INDIVIDUALS
WITHOUT WHOM THE AUDIO PORTION OF THE PROJECT WOULD NOT HAVE BEEN POSSIBLE:
Jeff Hixon, John Watkin, Eamon Harrington, the staff of Planet Grande Pictures, VoiceBox and
VoiceBank.net, Jill Cheris, Dennis Contreras, David Kelly, Erica Kelly, Amber Dahlin, Stewart Wilson-Turner,
Roger Tallman, Lynn Tallman, Mike Harvey, NBC Studios, Harpo Productions, Michele Weir,
and all of the instrumental and vocal musicians who helped bring this score to life.

The Tales

Little Red Riding Hood 13

Iris Brown 15
A loving mother who needs her daughter out of the house
Glenn Close & Kevin Hawkes

Wolf von Big Baden 17
A predator with a taste for little children and polyester nightgowns
Robin Williams & Tony DiTerlizzi

Woodcutter Gunderson 19
A folksy do-gooder with an ax to grind
Bruce Willis & Steve Johnson & Lou Fancher

Alberta Louise Johnson 21
A bedridden granny who's more gutsy than she ever imagined
Oprah Winfrey & Jerry Pinkney

Hannah Milner Primrose Red Brown 23
An adventurous girl with poor focus
Lisa Kudrow & David Catrow

The Frog Prince 25

Princess Isabelle von Trifle 27
A spirited girl with a frog in her moat
Minnie Driver & Mary Engelbreit

Hexed 29
A bug-eyed frog who's a prince of a guy
Steven Spielberg & Berkeley Breathed

H.R.H. Ermintrude Brunhilda Katerina Liliana III 31
A queen of a mother in whom honesty reigns
Barbra Streisand & Keith Graves

The Princess's Pillow 33
A silent witness; to believe she's just another pretty pillow is simply a sham
Martha Stewart & Cynthia von Buhler

Prince Blomqvist von Saunabaden 35
A boy desperate for a kiss before he croaks
Hugh Grant & J.otto Seibold

Goldilocks and the Three Bears 37

Goldilocks 39
A little home invader . . . or an innocent girl just looking for a phone?
Calista Flockhart & Giselle Potter

Ted E. "Papa" Bear 41
A ferocious grizzly with a soft heart and a soft belly
Gen. H. Norman Schwarzkopf & Chris Van Allsburg

Cosentina Molly "Mama" Bear 43
A controlling bearfem disturbed to find her disarray gone thisaway
Whoopi Goldberg & Chris Raschka

Owen "Baby" Bear 45
A brave little cub whose stuff has been messed with!
Conan O'Brien & David Shannon

Rumplestiltskin 47

The Farm Girl's Father 49
A hay man who adores his daughter and thinks quite highly of himself
Kevin Kline & Anita Lobel

H.R.H. William Savage Fairborne 51
A wise king in pursuit of the most valuable riches for his son
Kelsey Grammer & Stephen T. Johnson

The Spinning Wheel 53
A spunky soul trapped in a life of dull turns . . . until now
Jennifer Love Hewitt & Istvan Banyai

Rumplestiltskin 55
A strange little man with a strange little plan
Mike Myers & Daniel Adel

Giselle 57
A sweet farm girl who spins gold and becomes queen . . . but at what cost?
Gwyneth Paltrow & Michael Paraskevas

Victor Shade Fairborne 59
A handsome young king with an odd story to tell
Nicolas Cage & Barry Moser

Olivia Opal 61
A most perceptive and precious baby princess, the jewel of her mother's heart
Hallie Kate Eisenberg & Mary GrandPré

Once Upon a Fairy Tale

Little Red Riding Hood

Iris Brown

AS TOLD BY GLENN CLOSE

Illustrated by Kevin Hawkes

I wanted to surprise my treasured daughter Primrose Red with the perfect pair of leggings to match her beloved red riding hood. It had taken me weeks to carefully appliqué them with deep red velvet roses. In fact, I finished the very night before her birthday and tucked them into my sewing basket to wrap first thing in the morning. But when I awoke, I was horrified to discover that a mouse had found its way into my things and chewed away half of the roses! I had to get Red out of the house so I could secretly repair everything in time for her birthday dinner, so I asked her to deliver my weekly basket of parsnip soup and biscuits to Granny.

I must admit I felt a bit anxious about letting Red go alone. She's wonderfully curious, however I fear her adventurous spirit can lead her into trouble. But the sky was sunny, the birds were singing their hearts out, and it was her birthday, after all. She was growing up. It was time to have faith and do a little letting go.

Red's vivid blue eyes sparkled with excitement from behind her gold-rimmed glasses. "Don't speak to strangers," I cautioned as I handed her Granny's basket. "And don't dawdle. I want you back before dark. Above all," I warned, "never stray from the path."

As Red skipped away, I remembered the rose soap I'd meant to send Granny. I caught up with her at the end of our walk and placed it in the basket, then watched until I saw the last flash of her red hood disappear into the wood. Turning back toward our cottage, I noticed something glimmering on our doorstep. Red's glasses! I ran up the path calling after her but the woods answered only with the sound of leaves rustling in the breeze.

I took a deep breath. Red knew the route by heart. "Have faith," I thought. "Let go." I closed my eyes, wished my girl well, and prayed she'd stay on the path until she was safely knocking on Granny's bright blue door.

Wolf von Big Baden

AS TOLD BY ROBIN WILLIAMS

Illustrated by Tony DiTerlizzi

A wolf of my stature deserves a nutritious meal every now and then . . . and there is nothing quite as tasty or good for you as a tiny girl in a red cape. I can't live on three little pigs alone. What do you expect me to eat? Nuts and berries? Hello, food chain!

So I was sunbathing in the woods when this fabulous snack came skipping down the path. Did I say snack? I meant little girl in a red riding cape. Now, most wolves would eat without saying "hello," but I insist on being courteous with children before I devour them. A little get-to-know-you . . . then it's lunchtime. "Good day, little girl," I chimed.

She turned and said, "Hello," to a tree! This girl needed glasses like I needed a hot meal.

"Over here." I waved my claws. "What's your name?"

"Red—" she said, then mumbled something about how her mother had told her never to talk to strangers.

"I am Wolf von Big Baden." I bowed. "Pleased to meet you. I'm no longer a stranger." She seemed very afraid. *I loved that!* She quickly explained she was off to visit her sick grandmother who lived deep in the woods, then excused herself. Normally, I would've gobbled her up right then and there. But I figured, why not make this a grand feast: munch Granny first . . . and save the red dumpling for dessert! So I let her go. I knew the house she was talking about; it always had a basket of muffins piled in the trash out back. I took the high road. Red took the low road. I knew I'd get to Granny's before her.

I swallowed the old lady in one big gulp. My mother always warned me to chew my food for better digestion, but did I listen? *Uh*, the heartburn! Anyway, I disguised myself in one of Granny's nightgowns—I must say, I was stunning—then leaped under her bedcovers just as Red knocked on the door. My stomach growled in anticipation. "Come in!" I called in a high voice. This was going to be fun: dinner and a show!

Woodcutter Gunderson

As told by Bruce Willis

Illustrated by Steve Johnson & Lou Fancher

Working deep in the woods splitting timber and firewood, I don't see a lotta folks. But I'm never lonely. The forest creatures are my friends, except them nasty critters that prey on helpless little animals. They really peeve me. Why, I'd do anything to even the score between the likes of the lambs and the wolves. Just thinking about it makes me swing my axes like some crazed Samurai guy: "Beware of Gundersen, the big man with two axes!"

My whooping was cut off by the happy sound of Li'l Red singing and skipping. She was carrying real pretty wildflowers and a nice wicker basket. I hadn't seen her in some time, but I'd never forget that little girl. She always wore red and was so polite when she and her mama passed by on their way to her granny's house. But today, two things struck me as kinda odd. Red was squinting up her eyes a whole lot . . . and she was alone. Of course she was a little older now and it was none of my business, but I was just a bit surprised her mama had let her travel out here alone.

I didn't want to scare Red, but I had to warn her to be mindful. These woods are filled with dangers! She gave me "that look" like she felt too smart to listen to the likes of me, then told me some story about how she'd already met up with a wolf and handled him just fine. I didn't believe her, of course, but I didn't tell her that. I just strongly suggested she move along quick and direct-like. She thanked me and went on her way.

"What a brave little girl," I thought. But then I thought of my three little girls at home. There was no way in creation I'd *ever* let them travel alone in these woods no matter how confident they pretended to be! I stopped my chopping and ran after Red to see her safely to Granny's. I only hoped I could catch her. She was a fast one!

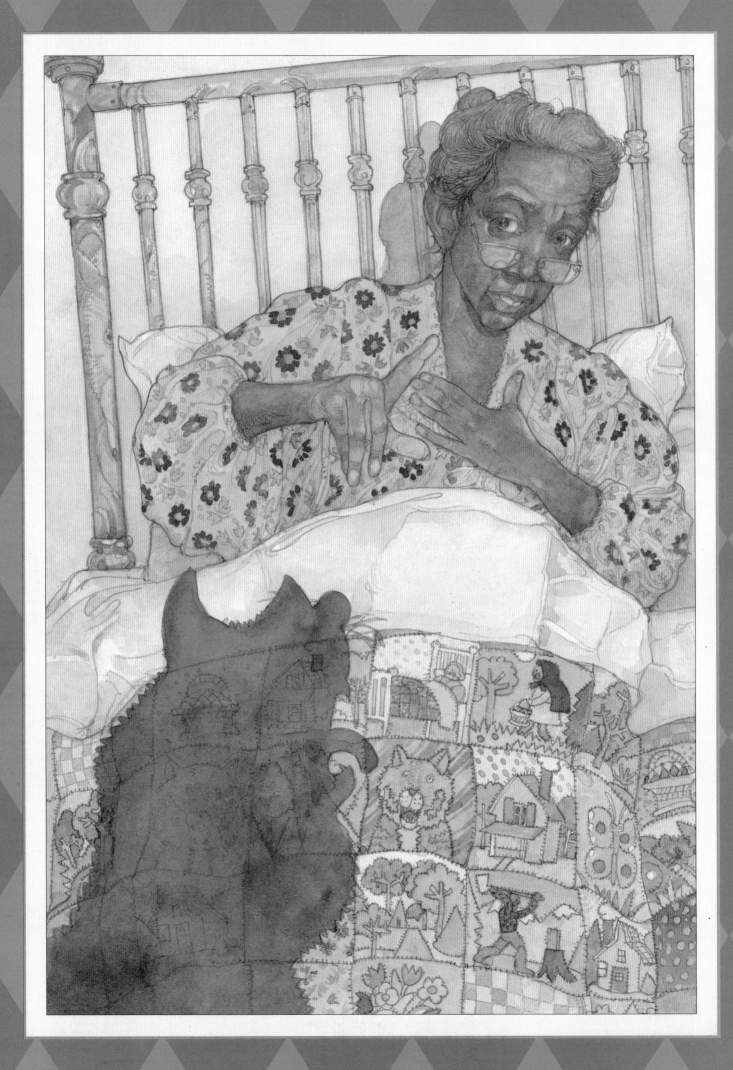

Alberta Louise Johnson

AS TOLD BY OPRAH WINFREY

Illustrated by Jerry Pinkney

At 72, I'm an attractive lady. I eat healthy, tend my own vegetable garden, and walk three miles to church each and every Sunday. So I don't understand how, living so well, I took to feeling so poorly. The doctor even ordered me to bed! I hate feeling shut in, but I do look forward to the weekly visits from my daughter and the occasional treat of seeing my grandbaby, Primrose Red (that girl never calls, but she e-mails). It'd been quite a while since I'd seen Red. I was expecting her that afternoon, and right on time, I heard her sweet voice echoing through the house.

Now, what I believe I've neglected to mention is that on that very day, I had found myself *inside the belly of a wolf!* I'd been swallowed up before I knew it. I was angry and confused, and crowded into his dark, messy, overheated guts. It was not very nice at all. And honestly, I just couldn't help thinking I'd spent my entire life trying to eat healthy and do the right things, only to find myself feeling poorly and being eaten by a wolf! What was that all about?! But my thoughts and worries quickly returned to Red. The wolf had already eaten me, and although I was just a nice size twelve, there wasn't much room left in his stomach for her. I feared he might only eat part of her, then leave her for dead!

I kicked and hollered from inside, "Reeeeddd, run for your life!" But my carrying on just sounded like a lot of belly grumbling and did little more than make that wolf burp a whole lot. All I could do was wait in there and pray and listen to Red's voice. Now let me say this: I wasn't especially happy with what I heard her say! How on God's great green earth could Red think–even for a second–that the big, ugly, hairy, burping, overgrown dog in my nightie was her fine-looking granny? *What was wrong with that girl?!*

Hannah Milner Primrose Red Brown

AS TOLD BY LISA KUDROW

Illustrated by David Catrow

The optometrist calls my eyesight "horrible." I say the world's a more interesting place when it's blurry. Besides, I hate how I look in glasses. I hadn't even realized I'd forgotten them when I got to Gran's cottage. I peeked into her room on my way to the kitchen. She looked a lot worse than hot soup and muffins could cure, but I tried to seem casual. "Gran, your eyes seem abnormally large," I began. I was thinking, "Thyroid disorder?" but was further distracted by her big nose. No disease I knew included bulging eyes and enormo-nose! Gran must've sensed my distress, because she smiled gently. Her teeth were jagged!

Wait. "It sort of looks like Gran . . ." I thought, "but something's weird." *Where are my glasses?* The growl, "*I'm going to eat you alive!*" made me realize the glasses were my least concern. This was that wolf I'd seen on the road! I grabbed the soup and sort of accidentally threw the whole boiling pot at his face. His mouth flew open but instead of a howl, *Gran* came flying out like she'd been shot from a cannon! The wolf was down, but not for good, and I had no plan. Should I leave Gran alone and try to fight a wolf? What if I lost? Maybe we could get swallowed whole and start a fire in his belly or something, like in *Pinocchio*?

Suddenly the woodsman burst through the door, axes swinging! The wolf tried to run, but before he was gone, so was his tail. We were saved! Of course the papers got it wrong. They hailed me as a hero when in truth, I ignored my mother's advice and put Gran and me in a lot of danger. I did, however, keep us alive long enough to get saved by the woodsman. That was good. And I do enjoy the sporty wolf-tail collar on my red coat, not to mention my new reputation. Instead of Daydreaming Little Red Riding Hood, I'm now the respected Big Bad Red Riding Hood . . . who's cool enough to wear her glasses.

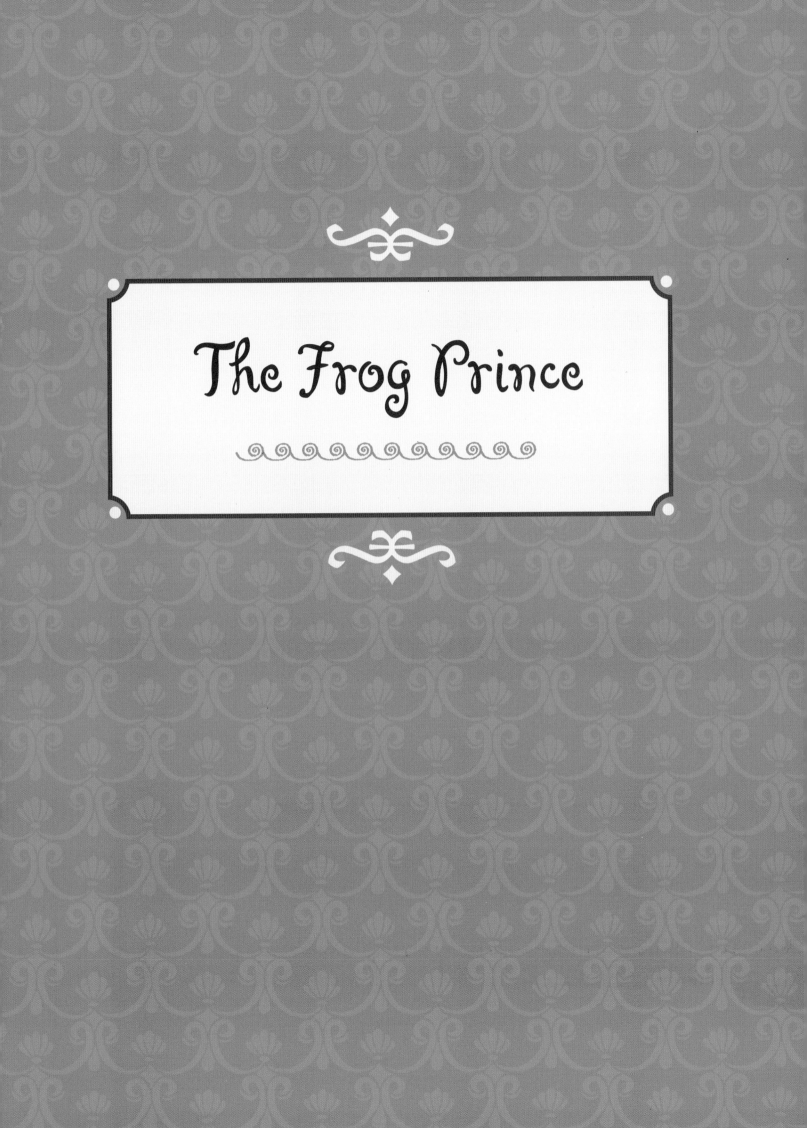

The Frog Prince

PRINCESS ISABELLE VON TRIFLE

Princess Isabelle von Trifle

AS TOLD BY MINNIE DRIVER

Illustrated by Mary Engelbreit

People can be so cruel. I must retreat to the privacy of our royal gardens to play with my dearest friend Hester because everyone laughs and whispers when they see me talking to her in the palace. You see, Hester is my doll. We were playing catch by the pond—well, I was throwing Hester high in the air and catching her— when it was as if she decided midair, "Time for a swim!" She plunged into the water and sank out of sight. Well, I've only learned to *lounge* by a pool not swim in one. "Hester, swim!" I screamed. "Somebody, anybody, please help!"

A croaky voice answered. Odd, but true: a big, slippery frog *spoke* to me from his lily pad, willing to help. "Quick," I commanded, "jump in! Save Hester! She has blonde hair and a pink dress; you can't miss her! For heaven's sake, I'll give you any- thing!"

"Listen," he said, "just let me be your friend, enjoy suppers together, have friendly sleepovers, and you know, hang out." Me, friends with a . . . frog? *Please!* And why would he want to be friends with *me?* I can't swim and I've actually *eaten* frog legs. One can't be friends with an entrée! But then, I *could* get Hester back if I just told Slimy what he wanted to hear. . . .

"Okay frog, I promise," I said, thinking of course, "Promise-schmomise!" The frog dove in straightaway and two seconds later Hester was at my feet. I grabbed her, then ran away as fast as I could. The faint "waaaaiiiittttt!" behind me gave way to a little voice inside my head: *A promise is a promise.* Ugh! My conscience! *Promises are made to be broken!* I reminded myself. The voice nagged on, *Isabelle von Trifle, you know what's right. . . .*

"Oh shut up voice, shut up shut up SHUT UP!" I shouted. "He's a *frog* for good- ness sakes! Surely he's already forgotten everything and carried on fly hunting, or whatever froggies do!" I forced his sorrowful bug-eyes out of my mind and hurried to the dining room to join Mother for supper.

Hexed

AS TOLD BY STEVEN SPIELBERG

Illustrated by Berkeley Breathed

Let me tell you, I'm more than a bug-eyed, tongue-flickin', fly-eatin' slug sucker. I'm a real prince! And if the right girl would give me the chance, I'd give her the world on a lily pad.

But pickings are slim around the bog, so I hopped to the pond at the palace. Rumor had it there was an interesting, beautiful, hard-to-get-to-know girl who lived there: the princess! I spotted her across the water. My heart leaped, and so did I—because at that exact moment, she dropped her doll into the pond. "Hey," I croaked. "Let me get that for you!"

"Thanks! I'll give you anything!" she gushed, which I think was pretty cool given she was royalty and I was, well, an amphibian.

"Just promise you'll be my friend," I said.

She laughed. "But you're a—"

I turned to jump away. "Then good-bye, Hester. . . ." I sang.

She almost fell into the water trying to stop me. "Fine, I'll be your friend!"

I dove in, plucked her doll out of a nest of green algae, and glided toward the surface. Through the sunlit, rippled water, the princess's face looked like a living oil painting. My stomach tingled in a way it hadn't since I'd gulped down that juicy three-ounce worm . . . but, ya know, different.

I came up, bowed my head, and laid the soggy doll at her feet. Her sweet voice rang out: "Thanks, frog!" But as I looked up, she was running away! *Ouch.* At the rate we're stepped on, my kind is on the verge of extinction. Not frogs—nice guys! Frankly, I didn't even know if I liked this girl, but I was determined: she was going to give me a chance, warts and all. I hopped after her at high speed until we reached a huge wooden door in the castle, which the lovely princess . . . *slammed* in my face! My heart thumped so hard in my chest, I looked like a belching bullfrog. I took a deep breath and knocked. And waited. And waited. And waited. And waited. . . .

H.R.H. Ermintrude Brunhilda Katerina Liliana III

AS TOLD BY BARBRA STREISAND

Illustrated by Keith Graves

1 am a good queen. Being a good mother is a much harder job. As I gazed at my little princess across our candlelit dining table, my mind began to wander. I want Isabelle to have a comfortable life, but most importantly I want her to be a good and happy person. Perhaps she does have a few too many ruby hair clips and ponies with braided tails. And she is not as patient as she could be. But she is so loving and energetic–

I was startled from my thoughts by an odd slurping sound, then a soft knock. Isabelle jumped up and opened the door. She gasped, then slammed it so hard my goblet of guava juice nearly tipped! I quietly waited for an explanation. My daughter sunk ever further into her chair until she hit bottom, and out the story came: She'd dropped her doll in the pond and asked a frog to rescue it. In exchange, the slimy thing was to be welcomed into our home as her friend.

Now, I strongly believe promises must be kept. It's a principle I've held dear since my tenth birthday, when the royal conjurer failed to produce the purple dog I was "promised." As my child, and as future queen, Isabelle must uphold the highest standards of decency–our feelings about slimy pond life aside. So beginning with my purple dog and ending with her regal position, I explained why she had to keep her promise to this frog.

"Guess who's coming to dinner?" I sighed, as together we welcomed our warty guest. What a simply charming, harmless creature! The frog rocked back on his heels and chatted cordially about history and nature and sport, then thanked us for our hospitality and asked to be shown upstairs.

"You are probably exhausted," I exclaimed. "Sweetheart, show Frog to your room." Isabelle made a terrible scowly face, which I pretended not to see. "Don't stay up all night giggling!" I called after her. I couldn't help but smile as I watched them disappear at the top of the stairs. "Good night, my love–"

The Princess's Pillow

As told by Martha Stewart

Illustrated by Cynthia von Buhler

For generations, my robin's-egg blue silk velvet cover has embraced the precious head of every princess who has lived in this castle as she's dreamed dreams, cried tears, or just slept peacefully through the night. My current princess is quite wonderful. She fluffs me all the time and loves every living creature. But I must say I was amazed—and disgusted—when she entered our bedchamber with a *frog* cupped in her delicate hands.

The frog's eyes were peculiarly . . . human . . . but I scarcely had time to think about how odd that was before he started nagging my princess to let him sleep on *me!* The thought undid my stuffing! Thankfully my princess was quite firm: I was a very special pillow for her use only! But the frog persisted. I nearly burst at the seams before she harshly banished him to the farthest corner of the bed. They both fell asleep quickly, but the frog was restless. I watched helplessly as he inched up, snuggling his warty body into me . . . right next to my princess's sleeping face! I was miserable.

Morning finally arrived. My princess opened her eyes to find herself cheek to cheek with the annoying creature. She was so startled that, without thinking, she picked him up and flung him! I had a nice chuckle over that, I must admit, but my princess felt terrible. She'd never want to hurt anything. She rushed over to comfort the fallen frog and quite unexpectedly—*ugh!*—planted a soft kiss on his slimy skin.

Suddenly, a stillness filled the room, shattered by a mysterious, silent explosion! When the smoke cleared, that ugly frog had transformed into *the most beautiful boy I'd ever seen!* He bowed his head and took my princess's hands in his own. Together, they dreamily propped their heads on me and began their friendship by sharing the stories of their lives. I proudly puffed up to my fullest, bolstered by the knowledge that yet again I was the centerpiece of a pivotal moment in our kingdom's history.

Prince Blomqvist von Saunabaden

AS TOLD BY HUGH GRANT

Illustrated by J.otto Seibold

My dad is a witch. It's quite embarrassing, really. Whenever I do something wrong, he puts a spell on me. I hadn't done much to deserve being turned into a frog. Just buried my little sister in the snow so my dog could practice avalanche rescue. We lost her for a day. She was all right. But Dad gave me three weeks as a frog with parole after two for good behavior, or kissing a princess. I developed a taste for small gnats and made friends with a jolly five-pound bullfrog named Serge who showed me to the palace grounds of Princess Pushy, who I'd heard was very beautiful.

Now, I hadn't realized I'd hopped in my sleep to her pillow after that lovely evening of nice food and conversation. I was so cozy. Until I found myself flying through the air and smacking into a wall! The impact left me cross-eyed, with double vision, as if two princesses were leaning over me with furrowed brows and ridiculous morning bed-head hair.

My eyes cleared as the princess lifted me in her hand . . . and kissed me. Her breath smelled of roses and Cherry Coke. Next thing I knew my froggy tongue was rolling in and out like a party trumpet sort of thing, I let out a massive *burp-ribbitt* and suddenly *I was a person again* . . . still standing on her hand, which must have been quite painful. I stepped back and apologized, then we both spoke at once. "What's that funny smell of pondweed?" she asked, wincing. And I: "Perhaps you'd like to borrow a comb?"

I've since discovered the princess's beauty is matched by her heart, which has grown far warmer since our meeting by the pond. We spend a lot of time in her castle, which keeps me safely out of reach of Dad's broomstick. And I've kept my frog mate Serge, who's now carried about by a footman on a velvet cushion. I'm certain that all of us are going to live quite happily ever after. Except the gnats. Sad to say, I'm still quite fond of snacking on them.

Goldilocks and the Three Bears

Goldilocks

AS TOLD BY CALISTA FLOCKHART

Illustrated by Giselle Potter

My folks always warned me about wandering too far from our house, and I usually listen. One time I didn't. But I had the coolest adventure that would never have happened if I'd followed the rules! I left home singing and skipping, and before I knew it, I was lost in the woods. I was just getting a little nervous when I found this oh-so-cute cottage. I knocked, thinking I'd use their phone to ring up my folks, but nobody was home. They don't call me Goldi*locks* for nothing; long story short, I "let myself in."

Three bowls of oatmeal were on the table, which I found a little bizarre, but I'd skipped breakfast and I was starving. I dug my spoon into the biggest bowl, but it was boiling hot, so I scooped a bite from the bowl next to it. It was cold–which, by the way, is totally gross. The smallest bowl had sweet little swirls of brown sugar on top and just a hint of steam. It was perfect! It's rude to eat standing, so I went to sit down. I couldn't reach the seat of the biggest chair. The next chair was so soft and squishy that the cushion practically swallowed me and I got claustrophobic. The last chair was perfect, but it must have been poorly made, because I'm just a little thing, and when I sat on it, it broke into a million pieces, which made me feel rotten. I tried to put it back together but I'm not exactly mechanically inclined, you know.

Anyway, I decided to look upstairs for the phone. Between my attempted wood-working and the stairway hike, I was worn out. When I saw three beds all I could think was N-A-P. I flopped down on the littlest bed, and I think I fell asleep. My mind drifted from imagining what kind of people had three sizes of everything and–*hello*–no phone, to flying snakes and marionettes and clouds and . . . Did I hear footsteps? Oh, I was so comfy, *yawn*, it was just part of my dream. Or maybe it was real . . . *yawn* . . . I didn't care. . . .

Ted E. "Papa" Bear

AS TOLD BY GEN. H. NORMAN SCHWARZKOPF

Illustrated by Chris Van Allsburg

When danger dares to cross my path, I stretch to my majestic twelve-foot height, thrash my fearsome four-inch claws, and roar a sharp-toothed growl backed by every ounce of my one thousand pounds. But I don't do it often. Mama Bear doesn't like it when I raise my voice. She likes my teeth better when I smile . . . which makes me smile a lot. The other thing Mama isn't fond of is my big belly, and aw, she's right. A few hundred extra pounds does call for a large dose of discipline, diet, and exercise. I just don't care much for exercise. In fact, on the morning of "the Incident" I'd fixed some high-fiber oatmeal and set it on the table, hoping to get out of our morning walk. Mama sweetly thanked me . . . then insisted we hit the road and enjoy breakfast when we came back. How could I argue? She and my boy were willing to join me in my battle of the bulge, and along the way Mama generously ignored my checking the beehives for honeycomb, looking under logs for moth larvae, and grabbing treats from picnic garbage cans. Our walk went fine. But when we returned home, we found our front door ajar.

Blackie Bear! That miserable runt had raided our refrigerator before. He must've been poking around and smelled our breakfast on the table! His evidence was everywhere: he'd picked at our oatmeal, licked my little boy's bowl clean, and—worst of all—moved my chair! *No one* touches Ted E. Bear's special chair!

I heard a noise and we pounded upstairs to find a Blackie-shaped lump snoring under *Baby Bear's blankets!* How dare that bear hibernate in my son's bed! As I thundered toward him, my big black snout was assaulted by the strangest scent, but I was already pulling off the covers when it hit me that it wasn't Blackie's normal stink. It caught me off guard. I couldn't even get my fierce growl going before it was too late: I was face-to-face with the beast!

Cosentina Molly "Mama" Bear

As told by Whoopi Goldberg

Illustrated by Chris Raschka

Peace and a piece of heaven to me is playing my cello and enjoying my family. We stay fit on a diet of love and togetherness and walk half a mile every morning. But the oddest thing happened when we got home from our walk the other day. First off, our front door was wide open. Truth be told, I rarely lock our door. Friends and family like to drop by here and there, whether we're here or there, and I want a home where everyone feels welcome. But next I noticed that the oatmeal we'd left on the table had been picked at. Of course, our food has been disturbed before: a Russian cousin of mine once stopped in and made himself at home, but who could blame him? Papa's cooking is hard for any bear to resist. But *then* I noticed our chairs had been moved and BB's chair was smashed to pieces. This looked like my brother Zion's doing. He's a big bear with a big appetite. But if Zion broke something, he would've left a note. . . .

Just then, my nose began to tickle with an odd scent. It smelled . . . like danger. Situations like this are rare in our peaceful lives, but when they crop up, I'm not the higgledy-piggledy type. Without a word, my eyes met Papa's. I grabbed BB's hand—hopeful he'd picked up something from those karate lessons—and we climbed the stairs. That's when things really began to get ugly.

Straightening the bed is just something I can't stand to do. I'm all about comfortable chaos. My things were in standard hurricane condition when I left, but now my sheets were neat, the pillows fluffed, and the week's *New York Times* neatly stacked by the bed! No one I knew or cared for would do such a thing! The danger smell grew stronger as my eye caught the big lump on BB's bed. *What was under there?!* I grabbed my cello to whack at it, but then kept my head and looked to Papa to make the next move—

Owen "Baby" Bear

AS TOLD BY CONAN O'BRIEN

Illustrated by David Shannon

Mom says I've got the blackest nose in the forest, which means I'll be a great hunter someday, like my dad. Dad caught a bobcat once. During our walk he told me how he'd swallowed it in one gulp—which made me hungry for breakfast. When we came home we found our door open. I figured a rabbit had snuck inside. This was my chance! I bent into a hunting crouch. See, my name's Owen but my family calls me "Baby Bear." It's okay in private, but I hate when they say it in front of other cubs. If I could prove myself and catch that rabbit for supper, maybe I'd never hear the name "Baby Bear" again! I pushed past Dad to get inside.

Now, I love to play with my food, and this morning's oatmeal had been no exception. I'd made cream rivers, butter houses, and sugar mountains, then made a storm with my spoon and mixed it up. But my creation . . . was *gone*. Then I saw my chair. I loved that chair. It was *broken* into a million pieces! This was no rabbit. Something big was in our house. Maybe even a bobcat.

We couldn't believe what we saw when we got upstairs. Everything was messed up. The blankets on *my bed*, which I make carefully so there's no room for monsters to sneak in, were all pushed into a big lump . . . which suddenly . . . *moved!* Dad's paws were shaking—I guess he was cold—but he yanked off the covers. A bad smell hit me, and then I saw it: I'd never faced a human before! It was making horrible, loud shrieking sounds, and before any of us could even think, it ran down the steps and was gone. I asked Dad why he always said all humans are fierce killers—this one looked so afraid! He just said it was a good thing he was around to scare it off and that maybe I shouldn't ask so many questions. The house was a mess and Mom and Dad were pretty freaked out. But I was excited. I knew this meant we'd get pizza tonight!

Rumplestiltskin

The Farm Girl's Father

AS TOLD BY KEVIN KLINE

Illustrated by Anita Lobel

I'm the hay man. I deliver hay to the royal stable. It's not a grand job. Of course, without my hay there would be no horses . . . which would mean no real hunting and certainly no foreign wars. Surely without me, the entire kingdom would grind to a halt! And so I humbly serve.

When I heard the king was searching for the perfect girl to marry his son the prince, it was as if he were calling out to me. You see, I have a daughter. In fact, I call her Princess. She's sweet, clever, brilliant—a genius, really. I'm not bragging; I can't help but see Princess for what she is. So when the king visited the stables to admire my hay—or possibly, his horses—I couldn't allow him to miss the opportunity to hear about my daughter. I simply began talking about her in a voice loud enough for him to hear if he chose to. He seemed to be ignoring me. So I found myself saying, "She can whistle under water. She can throw a pig through a doughnut." Nothing. Finally, I exclaimed, "She can spin straw into gold!"

Apparently, royalty has no sense of humor when it comes to gold. Silly king. And silly me . . . for now I had to go home and tell my daughter what I'd done. "You said *what*? I could spin straw into gold!" she cried.

"Yes," I said. "Can you, by the way?" She glared. I had to ask, especially in light of the king's decree that he would chop off my head if she couldn't do it. Clearly it hadn't occurred to him that such an action would seriously hinder my ability to deliver hay and thus threaten his kingdom's very existence. "You can do anything if you put your mind to it," I urged my daughter as I took her into my arms. "I only want you to be happy. And royal." Hoping for the best, I watched her ride off toward the castle . . . and rubbed my vulnerable neck.

H.R.H. William Savage Fairborne

AS TOLD BY KELSEY GRAMMER

Illustrated by Stephen T. Johnson

hat a magnificent young prince that boy has become!" I mused as my son thundered by on his marvelous stallion. He will make a fine king. But what I truly desire for him is a lifetime of love with a strong, caring bride at his side. Certainly he'll have plenty to say about who he marries. I'd never force my will on him. We'll know her when we find her—er—*he'll* know her when we find her—

My thoughts were interrupted by the booming voice of the stable's hay man. I always listen to my subjects; they are the life's blood of the land. He was bragging that his daughter could spin straw into gold! I do not tolerate lying, and certainly this boast was a lie. But it captured my attention. How might this girl respond to her father's claims? I ordered him to send her to the palace at once.

On first sight she was attractive, but rather plain. Then as she spoke it became clear she was a rare beauty, sparkling with keen intellect and a royal nature. I liked her. Dare I say, she reminded me of . . . me. "You have until sunrise to spin this straw into gold," I explained. "If you can't do it, you and your boastful father will suffer dire consequences!" I didn't intend to carry out my threats. A father's love isn't a crime. Truly, had it meant my son's happiness, I might have boasted my kingdom to be made of diamonds.

Astonishingly, before my very eyes, this girl spun something far more precious than gold: she simply bowed her head and said she understood. She could've declared her father a liar to save herself. Instead she preserved his honor, demonstrating character beyond measure. At that moment she delivered on her father's promise . . . and won my heart. But I didn't let on just yet. I headed off for a well-deserved nap, wondering what she'd say by morning, and what my son would think of this extraordinary girl. What lovely children they could make!

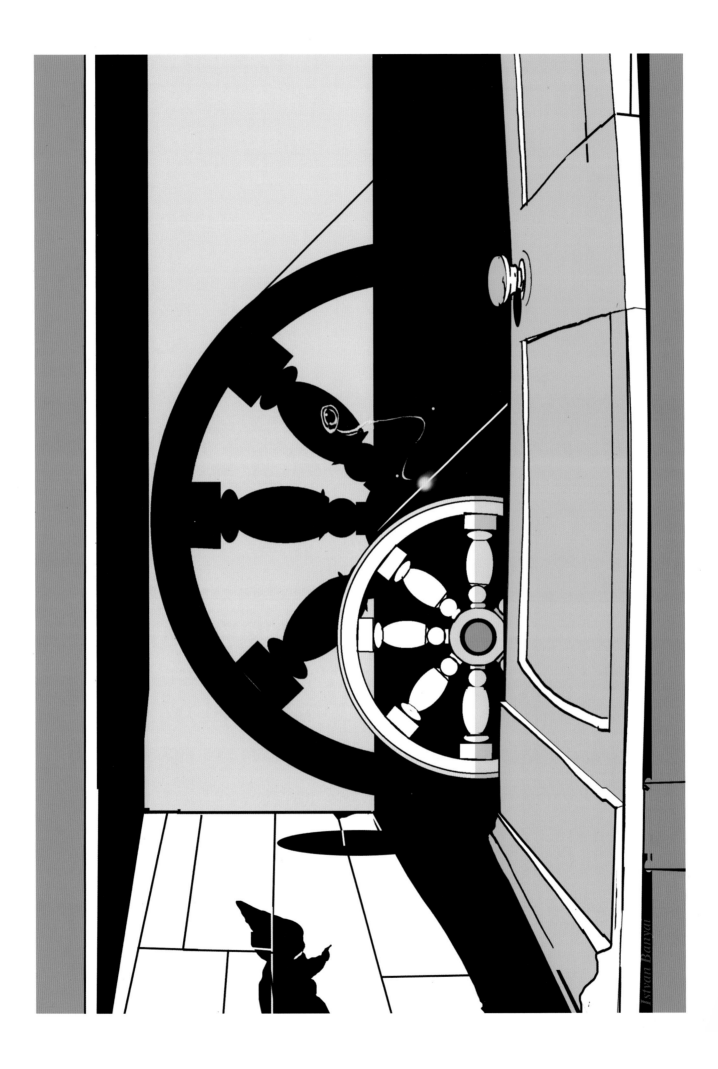

The Spinning Wheel

As told by Jennifer Love Hewitt

Illustrated by Istvan Banyai

Face it: I'm an inanimate object. Every day, up early, spin a few yards, then sit in the corner. It's a boring life. But things took an interesting turn when Royal Page Albert showed up and dumped a pile of straw around me. Next came the king himself, followed by a beautiful farm girl. The king demanded she spin that straw into . . . *gold!?* I almost bust my bobbin laughing. *Straw?* Into *gold?* What a riot! The girl started crying when he left. Poor little sister. If I had arms, I'd have given her a hug.

Just then, an odd gnome fella sprang in and announced *he* could spin straw into gold. He grabbed the locket from the girl's neck and sat at me to work. His gnarly fingers worked at lightning speed. The straw hummed through me, melting into liquid that he blew and twisted into threads of *gold!* It made me giddy. Then he disappeared.

The king was shocked. "More gold!" he demanded. At the snap of the king's fingers, Albert hauled in ten more bales of straw. I was glad—I was hoping for another feel-good session with freaky guy . . . but the girl was pretty wigged out. When troll man returned, she gave him the only other thing she owned: a tin ring that belonged to her mother. In minutes, gold was everywhere.

The king couldn't *believe* she'd done it again! He sent us to a straw-filled barn in the middle of nowhere—so she "couldn't rely on any tricks"—and said he wanted to see mounds of gold!

Now, I can't weave the big guy's thoughts, but it seemed this whole thing wasn't about gold to him. After just two days of being surrounded by the shiny stuff, even *I* was starting to tire of it—like chocolate, it's great, but you don't want it every day. I could only imagine how a bizillionaire king might feel! He was clearly after something more precious. I just hoped that in her desperation to deliver it, that sweet girl wouldn't give up something she'd later regret!

Rumplestiltskin

AS TOLD BY MIKE MYERS

Illustrated by Daniel Adel

I'm classically grotesque. I'm four feet tall, I have mange rot, and my breath smells like manure and feet. It's like I fell from the ugly tree and hit every branch on the way down. Truly. I'm hideous. But most of all, I'm lonely. The chances of me finding a long-term relationship with anybody are slim. The chance of me having kids: about none. When I was born, the doctor slapped my mother. I'm gross! But I'd so love a tiny person looking up to me as "Dad" and lifelong friend. *Sigh*.

Anyway, in my spare time–ugly trolls have lots of it–I started spinning straw into hay. I wasn't making a cent. Eventually, I developed a magical process, and it was like I'd stumbled into a gold mine: "Hayenic Alchemic Counterprocessing." In plain English, I could spin straw into gold.

When my ear hair picked up vibes that there was a maiden in distress who might become the heir-producing queen if she could *spin straw into gold*, I knew this was the chance for *both of us* to get what we wanted. I'd help her . . . in exchange for her firstborn child! She could always have more! I zapped myself to the castle.

I don't exactly have a way with the ladies. I chickened out of asking this gorgeous girl for what I really wanted. Twice. I just swapped whatever trinket she had for spinning the gold and pretended I didn't want anything else. But when the king moved her to a straw-filled barn for a final "test," I knew it was my last shot. I asked for the kid. The girl knew if she didn't deliver gold, the king was going to off her dad. High drama. She struck the deal last minute, just as the king's horses were approaching.

Look, there was a chance the prince and this girl wouldn't even like each other, let alone get married and have babies. We made a fair deal. No guilt! I vanished, off to patiently wait for the Happy Birthday. Me: nearly a dad!

Giselle

AS TOLD BY GWYNETH PALTROW

Illustrated by Michael Paraskevas

Blessed with a loving husband and a beautiful new daughter, my life could not have been more wonderful. Sounds of celebration echoed through the castle as I set my happily gurgling Olivia in her cradle. I treasured the moment. But suddenly, I was overcome with the eerie feeling of being watched.

I turned and my heart sank. The little man had returned. I couldn't give him my daughter. I knew that without his help I might never have met my husband or had Olivia, but even trapped as I felt amidst those piles of hay I should *never* have lost sight of how my promise could shape my future! I frantically offered him castles, jewels, fine horses, anything. He waved me off. Then, oddly, he appeared to feel a twinge of guilt. He offered me three chances to fairly undo my promise! But as he explained the "game," my heart sank again. How could I guess his name?

I blurted, "Robert, Arthur, Henry–"

"Uh-uh," he sang, a grin creeping across his face.

"Charles, Edward!" I tried.

"No, no, *no!*" he shouted. In a puff of smoke, the little man, and my first chance to guess his name, were gone.

The next evening I gazed longingly at my tiny princess. A sharp breeze cut the air. He was back. I tried to stay calm; only two chances remained. An odd man might have a peculiar name. . . . "Balthazar, Cornelius, Zebedee–" I began.

He wagged his finger. "No!" I grew so frustrated, so angry!

"Spartacus, Lysander, Orlando." He giggled then vanished again. Just one chance left!

Heartbroken, I held Olivia close. I found comfort only in the thought of my husband, due to return from the hunt that evening. Perhaps our love could somehow overpower the little man's magic and ensure our baby would remain with us forever?! As if he heard my thoughts, at that instant I heard my husband's whistled song drawing even nearer in the hall. He opened the door and I turned to face him. For the first moment in days, my tears paused.

Victor Shade Fairborne

As told by Nicolas Cage

Illustrated by Barry Moser

Around my twentieth birthday, my father began his campaign to help choose a wife for me. Every well-heeled noblewoman was dragged to our castle, but the last thing I wanted was a boring regal marriage to some society cream puff. *If* I married, I wanted a girl with whom I could be myself, and I'd always imagined I'd find her myself. But then surprisingly Father explained he'd met a simple farm girl who I might find interesting. We arranged a casual meeting in the gardens.

For me it was love at first sight. She was gorgeous, though her magic ran deeper. In her eyes I saw the edge of the universe . . . and when she started joking about the royal guards, I knew I'd found my soul mate. I wanted to slay a dragon for her right then and there!

Just when I thought life couldn't be any happier, little Olivia arrived in our lives. I was at peace inside and out. Sword fighting could never come close to the thrill of dancing with my baby in my arms.

I went off to hunt for the feasts in celebration of Olivia's birth and I missed her and her mother terribly while I was gone. I ran to the nursery the moment our party returned to the castle. I couldn't wait to hold my daughter and to share the strangest story with my wife. Deep in the woods, I'd seen an odd-looking little man dancing in circles. I'm sure he was some kind of lunatic. He was chanting a bizarre sort of nursery rhyme that went something like this:

Oh, I am Rumplestiltskin!
The cat could've never gotten out, if she hadn't let him in!
Need gold or scrap or tin?—I'll spin!
A child is the prize I win!

Oddly, my wife erupted into laughter and tears at my story. Did she find it funny? Perhaps she was just emotional because she missed me, as I missed her. It didn't matter. I held her close, glad to be home.

Olivia Opal

AS TOLD BY HALLIE KATE EISENBERG

Illustrated by Mary GrandPré

As a newborn baby, I can only see things close up. I can just about focus on the mobile of golden crowns dangling above me while I hug my soft pink blankie and drift in and out of sleep. I notice stuff like that my feet are smaller than my mother's thumbs. But my favorite thing is to stare at my mother's beautiful face. When she holds me her eyes sparkle, her hair glistens like gold, and her kisses make me feel safe and warm. But when Mom cuddled me this evening, something was wrong. A tear ran down her rosy cheek. *What did I do to make her happiness go away?*

Just then, my father bounded into the room. He always makes the corners of Mom's mouth go up. He'd get her happiness back! He gathered us up in his strong arms and told us about his busy day. Mother hardly seemed to be listening . . . until he mentioned seeing a strange man named "Rumplestiltskin." With that word, everything changed. She laughed and cried happy tears and kissed Father all over his face. I don't know why the word made her so joyful, but I was glad it did. I dozed off to a peaceful sleep.

As Mother rocked me the next day, we had a visitor—a little man, not much bigger than me, but old and odd. He'd visited a few times before. Mother was never herself when he was around. "What's my name—last three guesses!" he snapped, darting around with fancy footsteps.

"Harvey," Mother said calmly.

"Nope." He laughed. "Not Harvey!"

"Stan, then," she tried. He giggled and snorted. I didn't understand what was going on, but it didn't seem good. Finally, *"Rumplestiltskin!"* she sang.

That word! It made people act so weird! At the sound of it, the little man got so angry, he twisted up and drilled himself into the floor! We never saw that little man again. No one ever spoke of him. And of course, Mother, Father, and I lived happily ever after, together.

The Cast

The Storytellers

FIROOZ ZAHEDI

Victor Shade Fairborne in *Rumplestiltskin*

NICOLAS CAGE is one of the most versatile actors of our time, who is equally well known for his poignant portrayals in drama and comedy. He is the winner of the 2001 ShoWest Distinguished Decade of Achievement in Film Award. He won an Academy Award for his performance in *Leaving Las Vegas*, and also received a Golden Globe, as well as Best Actor awards from the New York Film Critics Circle, the Los Angeles Film Critics Association, and the Chicago Film Critics for the role. Cage has starred in a long string of successful films including *Gone in 60 Seconds, City of Angels, Face / Off, The Rock, Bringing out the Dead, Con-Air, Moonstruck*, and *Raising Arizona*.

Iris Brown in *Little Red Riding Hood*

GLENN CLOSE began her career on the stage, and continues her extremely successful Broadway theater career while carrying on a remarkable film career at the same time. She made her feature film debut in *The World According to Garp* in 1982, receiving an Academy Award nomination for her performance. She has received countless awards for her work, as well as five Academy Award nominations. Her films include *Fatal Attraction, Dangerous Liaisons, Hamlet, Air Force One,* and *101 Dalmatians*. Close also has a successful television career, with several Emmy and Golden Globe nominations and awards to her credit.

Princess Isabelle von Trifle in *The Frog Prince*

MINNIE DRIVER has achieved the unusual accomplishment of creating successful international careers in television, film, and theater. Her film credits include *An Ideal Husband, Good Will Hunting, Grosse Point Blank, The Governess*, and *Circle of Friends*. Her theater credits include performances in *Chatsky, Raving Beauties, A Comedy of Errors*, and *The School for Scandal*. Her television appearances include several productions for the BBC. She has also lent her voice to several animation projects, including *Tarzan, Princess Mononoke*, and *South Park: Bigger, Longer, and Uncut*.

Olivia Opal in *Rumplestiltskin*

HALLIE KATE EISENBERG is nine years old. She has appeared in several feature films, including *Paulie, The Insider, Bicentennial Man,* and *Beautiful.* Most recently she played Helen Keller in the acclaimed remake of *The Miracle Worker.* Well known for her work in Pepsi commercials, Hallie also played Christie in the highly regarded promos for the Independent Film Channel. Hallie serves as a special correspondent for *Entertainment Tonight* and has covered events such as the Gotham Awards, Nickelodeon Kids Choice Awards and the Emmy Awards.

Goldilocks in *Goldilocks and the Three Bears*

CALISTA FLOCKHART is best known for her portrayal of the complicated title character on the series *Ally McBeal.* Her performance in the role has earned her a Golden Globe and a People's Choice Award. Her film credits include *A Midsummer Night's Dream, Telling Lies in America,* and *Things You Can Tell Just by Looking at Her.* Her theater credits include *The Glass Menagerie* and *Three Sisters* on Broadway and numerous off-Broadway and regional productions.

Cosentina Molly "Mama" Bear in *Goldilocks and the Three Bears*

WHOOPI GOLDBERG has won numerous awards and considerable acclaim for her work in film, television, and theater. She earned an Academy Award nomination and a Golden Globe Award for her film debut in *The Color Purple,* and she won an Academy Award and a Golden Globe for her performance in *Ghost.* Her film career spans over forty movies, including *Sister Act, Boys on the Side,* and *Girl, Interrupted.* Goldberg has also made her mark as the executive producer of shows including the Emmy Award-winning *Hollywood Squares* and the Lifetime series *Strong Medicine.* Goldberg has been honored with multiple NAACP Image Awards and is the author of two books, *Alice* and *Book.*

H.R.H William Savage Fairborne in *Rumplestiltskin*

KELSEY GRAMMER is a three-time Emmy Award–winning actor who portrays Dr. Frasier Crane on the top-rated comedy series *Frasier*. Grammer first introduced the character in 1984 on the hit series *Cheers*. He has also had great success in theater and film. His theater credits include *Richard II* and *Quartermaine's Terms*, as well as Broadway performances of *Macbeth* and *Othello*. Grammer's film credits include *Fifteen Minutes, Down Periscope,* and the voice of the prospector, Stinky Pete, in *Toy Story 2*.

Prince Blomqvist von Saunabaden in *The Frog Prince*

HUGH GRANT's acting credits are diverse and numerous, including performances in theater, television, and film. Grant became an international star in 1994 with his performance in *Four Weddings and a Funeral*, for which he won Golden Globe and British Academy Awards. Prior to that, he appeared in several films, garnering international acclaim for his performances. Grant's film credits include *Bridget Jones's Diary, Notting Hill, Mickey Blue Eyes, Sense and Sensibility,* and *Remains of the Day*. Grant's most recent project is a film version of Nick Hornby's *About a Boy*.

The Spinning Wheel in *Rumplestiltskin*

JENNIFER LOVE HEWITT was most recently seen in the hit comedy *HeartBreakers* with Sigourney Weaver. She has completed production on *The Devil and Daniel Webster* in which she plays the titular role of the Devil opposite Anthony Hopkins and Alec Baldwin. Her other featured credits include the smash hit *I Know What You Did Last Summer* and its sequel. Television audiences fell in love with her as Sarah Reeves on the hit series *Party of Five*. Additionally a talented singer/songwriter, Hewitt has had three successful solo albums. She resides in the Los Angeles area.

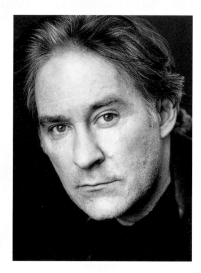

The Farm Girl's Father in *Rumplestiltskin*

KEVIN KLINE is an award-winning actor who has earned equal distinction in film and theater. He made his Broadway debut in Chekov's *The Three Sisters*, and has won Tony and Drama Desk Awards for his performances in *On the Twentieth Century* and *The Pirates of Penzance*. Kline began his film career in *Sophie's Choice* and went on to appear in films such as *The Big Chill, Silverado, Dave,* and *In & Out*. Kline won an Academy Award for his work in *A Fish Called Wanda*.

Hannah Milner Primrose Red Brown in *Little Red Riding Hood*

LISA KUDROW is an Emmy Award-winning actress who is distinctly different from Phoebe Buffay, the character she portrays on the NBC hit comedy series *Friends*. Kudrow has received numerous awards and nominations for her television work. She has also received rave reviews and awards for her feature film work, which includes *The Opposite of Sex, Analyze This, Romy and Michele's High School Reunion, Mother, Clockwatchers, Hanging Up,* and *Lucky Numbers*. For her portrayal of Lucia in *The Opposite of Sex*, she won the Best Supporting Actress Award from the New York Film Critics, an Independent Spirit Award nomination, and a Chicago Film Critics Award nomination.

Rumplestiltskin in *Rumplestiltskin*

MIKE MYERS was born and raised in Toronto, where he began his career in the *Second City* comedy troupe. In 1989 he made his debut on *Saturday Night Live*, where he went on to receive an Emmy Award nomination for Best Performance in a Comedy or Variety Show and an Emmy Award for Best Writing for a Comedy or Variety Show. Myers's films include *Wayne's World, Wayne's World 2,* and *So I Married an Axe Murderer*, as well as the record-breaking smash hits *Austin Powers: International Man of Mystery* and *Austin Powers: The Spy Who Shagged Me*.

Owen "Baby" Bear in *Goldilocks and the Three Bears*

CONAN O'BRIEN is a man with "a comic identity as distinct as his name," according to the *New York Times*. In 2000, O'Brien entered his eighth season as writer, performer, interviewer, and host of the award-winning television show *Late Night with Conan O'Brien*. Since 1996 the show has consistently been nominated for the Emmy Award for Best Writing in a Comedy or Variety Series. In 1997 and 2000, O'Brien and the *Late Night* writing team won the Writer's Guild Award for Best Writing in a Comedy/Variety Series. O'Brien has also collaborated on writing sketches for *Saturday Night Live* and *The Simpsons*, for which he later became the supervising producer.

Giselle in *Rumplestiltskin*

GWYNETH PALTROW is a talented and respected actress who delighted the hearts of many in her award-winning performance as Viola de Lessups in the acclaimed box office hit *Shakespeare in Love*. Paltrow captured a Golden Globe Award, a Screen Actors Guild Award and an Academy Award for her performance in the film. Her other film credits include international box office hits *Emma, A Perfect Murder, Sliding Doors, Seven,* and *The Talented Mr. Ripley*. She currently resides in New York City.

Ted E. "Papa" Bear in *Goldilocks and the Three Bears*

GENERAL H. NORMAN SCHWARZKOPF, U.S. Army, Retired, has served in numerous command and staff assignments throughout the United States, Europe, and the Pacific. General Schwarzkopf is best known for his service as Commander in Chief, United States Central Command, and Commander of Operations for Desert Shield and Desert Storm. Since his retirement from the military, he has published a best-selling autobiography, *It Doesn't Take a Hero*, and participated in critically acclaimed television specials. General Schwarzkopf is chairman of the STARBRIGHT Foundation Capital Campaign.

Hexed in *The Frog Prince*

STEVEN SPIELBERG is a principal partner of DreamWorks SKG, and he has directed, produced, or been executive producer for seven of the twenty top-grossing films of all time, including *Jurassic Park*, and *E.T. the Extra-Terrestrial*. He received his first Academy Awards as producer and director of the 1993 film *Schindler's List* and earned his second Best Director Award for the 1998 film *Saving Private Ryan*. Spielberg has devoted much of his attention to philanthropic causes. He founded the Survivors of the Shoah Visual History Foundation, which has recorded over 50,000 Holocaust survivor testimonies, and he is the chairman of the STARBRIGHT foundation.

The Princess's Pillow in *The Frog Prince*

MARTHA STEWART's passion for creative and useful ideas and her constant encouragement to take pride in everyday living have made her America's most trusted guide to living with style. She is Chairman and CEO of Martha Stewart Living Omnimedia, an information-based company that creates original ideas for the home through its magazines, television show, web site, and merchandise. She has been named one of the Fifty Most Powerful Women by *Fortune* magazine and one of America's Twenty-Five Most Influential People by *Time* magazine.

H.R.H. Ermintrude Brunhilda Katerina Liliana III in *The Frog Prince*

BARBRA STREISAND—film director, actress, singer, and composer—is the only artist to achieve Oscar awards as both actress and composer, and Tony, Emmy, Golden Globe, Cable Ace, and Peabody Award honors. She has received the American Film Institute's Lifetime Achievement tribute and the National Endowment for the Arts' National Medal of Honor. Her directorial debut film, *Yentl*, earned her Golden Globes for director and producer, and *Prince of Tides* received a Directors Guild of America Best Director nomination, and seven Academy Award nominations. She is the best-selling female recording artist ever, with forty-three gold albums, twenty-seven platinum albums, and thirteen multi-platinum albums.

Alberta Louise Johnson in *Little Red Riding Hood*

OPRAH WINFREY has, through her multi-media corporation, grown to be one of the most influential voices of our time. She produces and hosts the award-winning *Oprah Winfrey Show*, the highest-rated talk show in television history. She has earned critical acclaim for her numerous acting roles, including an Academy Award nomination for her debut in *The Color Purple*. She is Founder and Editorial Director of *O, The Oprah Magazine*, which was named the most successful launch in magazine history.

Wolf von Big Baden in *Little Red Riding Hood*

ROBIN WILLIAMS is an Academy Award–winning, versatile actor who is known for his film career as well as his involvement with several humanitarian organizations. Williams garnered an Oscar for Best Supporting Actor for his performance in *Good Will Hunting*. He received Academy Award nominations for his work in *Good Morning Vietnam, Dead Poets Society*, and *The Fisher King*. He has appeared in thirty-five feature films, as well as in an Off-Broadway theater production of *Waiting for Godot*, and has received three Grammy awards, one for his recording of "Robin Williams Live at the Met." He has a long history of involvement with humanitarian organizations, including Comic Relief.

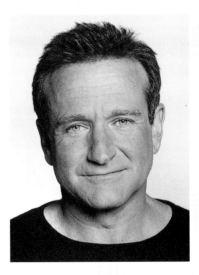

Woodcutter Gunderson in *Little Red Riding Hood*

BRUCE WILLIS has demonstrated incredible versatility and talent in a career ranging from action blockbusters to romantic comedies, earning him international acclaim. He enjoyed success with 1999's critically acclaimed box office smash *The Sixth Sense*, for which he earned a People's Choice Award for Best Actor. Willis's film credits include the successful *Die Hard* film series, *12 Monkeys*, and *Pulp Fiction*. Willis made his acting breakthrough in Sam Shepard's off-Broadway play *Fool for Love*, and went on to receive Emmy and Golden Globe awards for his role as David Addison in the hit television series *Moonlighting*.

Rumplestiltskin in *Rumplestiltskin*

DANIEL ADEL works as an illustrator and portrait painter in New York. His depictions of celebrities with very big heads (or very small bodies, depending on your perspective) have appeared in the pages of most of the magazines on a newsstand near you. He has painted portraits of CEOs, Chief Justices, and his mom. He has also painted carburetors, although he's not quite sure why.

The Spinning Wheel in *Rumplestiltskin*

ISTVAN BANYAI was born in Budapest in 1949. From 1972 until 1979 he worked in Hungary, creating drawings for posters and record sleeves and comic strips. In 1981 he moved to the United States, where his work has appeared in the *New Yorker, Time, Rolling Stone,* and many other publications. In 1995, Banyai illustrated the wordless picture book *Zoom,* which the *New York Times* and *Publishers Weekly* both named one of the best children's books of the year. *Zoom* was followed by *Re-Zoom* in 1996 and *R.E.M.: Rapid Eye Movement* in 1997. Abrams is currently publishing a book about Banyai's work titled *Minus Equals Plus*.

JODY BOYMAN

Hexed in *The Frog Prince*

BERKELEY BREATHED is a cartoonist, children's book author/illustrator, screenwriter, and director. His cartoon strip *Bloom County* with Opus the Penguin and Bill the Cat ran from 1980 to 1989 and was followed by *Outland,* which ran from 1989 to 1995. His cartoons were featured in 1,200 newspapers around the world. He has published eleven best-selling cartoon collections and five children's books. He is currently in development as writer and producer of two feature films based on his established characters. Breathed won the Pulitzer Prize for editorial cartooning in 1987.

Hannah Milner Primrose Red Brown in *Little Red Riding Hood*

DAVID CATROW is an artist whose work is sought by publishers, newspaper syndicates, and private collectors around the world. He has illustrated more than thirty books for children, and his editorial cartoons are syndicated to over nine hundred newspapers, including the *New York Times, USA Today,* and the *Washington Post*. His published picture books include *That's Good! That's Bad!* by Margery Cuyler, *The Million-Dollar Bear* by William Kotzwinkle, *Cesar's Amazing Journey* by Craig Hatkoff, and *She's Wearing a Dead Bird on Her Head!* by Katherine Lasky, which was named one of the *New York Times* Ten Best Illustrated Books of the Year. His most recent book is *Stand Tall Molly Lou Melon*, by Patty Lovell.

Wolf von Big Baden in *Little Red Riding Hood*

TONY DITERLIZZI (Dee-tur-lee-zee) is an award-winning child-genius prodigy (Honorable Mention in Mrs. Slowinsky's third grade Finger-Painting Challenge). His heroes include Norman Rockwell, Arthur Rackham, Dr. Seuss, that Roald Dahl guy, and Fozzie Bear. Author and illustrator of *Ted* and *Jimmy Zangwow's Out-of-This-World Moon Pie Adventure*, he has also doodled in *Alien and Possum, Ribbiting Tales,* and *Dinosaur Summer*. He rules the kingdom of Brooklyn, in the land of New York, with his wife Angela as queen, and their pug dog, Goblin. To see more of Tony's art, check out www.diterlizzi.com. *Nanu nanu!*

Princess Isabelle von Trifle in *The Frog Prince*

MARY ENGELBREIT, self-taught illustrator and pioneer in art licensing, is well known for her colorful, inspirational, and sometimes sassy designs, which adorn more than 6,500 products including greeting cards, calendars, books, and home accents. The "Queen of Cute" has a knack for capturing familiar moments that warm the hearts of enthusiasts around the world. Mary Engelbreit companies include an art licensing business, retail stores, and *Mary Engelbreit's Home Companion* magazine. Mary has illustrated 150 books, including her biography, *The Art and the Artist; The Snow Queen;* and *My Symphony*. See more of her art at www.maryengelbreit.com.

Olivia Opal in *Rumplestiltskin*

MARY GRANDPRÉ began her career as a conceptual illustrator for editorial clients. She has a successful career in many genres of illustration, from advertising, corporate, and editorial to children's books. She has been featured on the cover of *Time* magazine for her work with the *Harry Potter* series, and has worked on environment/scenery development in DreamWorks' animated film *Antz*. GrandPré has received national recognition and awards from the Society of Illustrators, *Communication Arts, Graphis, Print,* and *Art Direction*. She has illustrated six children's books and is currently working on her seventh.

H.R.H. Ermintrude Brunhilda Katerina Liliana III in *The Frog Prince*

KEITH GRAVES grew up in New Orleans, which explains a lot. He is a former javelin hurler and founder of the "Stupidism" art movement. Graves has written and illustrated *Frank Was a Monster Who Wanted to Dance, Pet Boy, Uncle Blubbafink's Seriously Ridiculous Stories,* and the upcoming *Three Nasty Gnarlies: A Smelly Opera.* He is the curator of the Keith Graves Happy Trash Art Gallery (http://vanguardfilms.com/happytrash/), father of twins Max and Emma, main squeeze of Nancy, and frontman of the sometimes-in-tune Whispering Javelinas . . . all at the same time. And he loves Barbra. Especially her poems.

Iris Brown in *Little Red Riding Hood*

KEVIN HAWKES has been an award-winning children's book illustrator for more than ten years and has worked on more than sixteen books, including most recently *Weslandia* by Paul Fleischman and *Marven of the Great North Woods* by Kathryn Lasky. Hawkes has also created book jackets, promotional materials, and artwork for various periodicals. He lives with his wife and children in Gorham, Maine.

KAREN HAWKES

H.R.H William Savage Fairborne in *Rumplestiltskin*

STEPHEN T. JOHNSON enjoys the challenge of projects that push his art and ideas to new heights. He has garnered numerous awards including gold and silver medals from the Society of Illustrators and was elected a master pastelist by the Pastel Society of America. His critically acclaimed books include *Alphabet City*, for which he received a Caldecott Honor Medal and a *New York Times* Ten Best Illustrated Books of the Year award; *City by Numbers; Hoops* and *Goal* by Robert Burleigh; and *On a Wintry Morning* by Dori Chaconas. His most recent creation is *My Little Red Toolbox*, a *Publishers Weekly* bestseller.

Woodcutter Gunderson in *Little Red Riding Hood*

STEVE JOHNSON & LOU FANCHER are a husband-and-wife team and the illustrators of many highly acclaimed books for children including Dr. Seuss's *My Many Colored Days*, Garrison Keillor's *Cat, You Better Come Home*, and Jon Scieszka's *The Frog Prince Continued*. Their recent book *I Walk at Night*, written by Lois Duncan, was recognized as one of the *New York Times* Ten Best Illustrated Books of 2000. Steve and Lou also provided set and character development for Pixar/Disney's *Toy Story* and *A Bug's Life*. They live with their son, Nicholas, in Minneapolis, Minnesota.

The Farm Girl's Father in *Rumplestiltskin*

ANITA LOBEL is an internationally successful picture book artist. She received a Caldecott Honor Medal for *On Market Street*. Lobel's 1998 memoir of her survival in Poland during the Nazi occupation, *No Pretty Pictures: A Child of War*, received high praise including being selected by the *New York Times* as one of the year's best books and being a finalist for the National Book Award. Her richly painted popular concept books include *Alison's Zinnia, Away from Home,* and most recently *One Lighthouse, One Moon*, which was one of the *New York Times* Ten Best Illustrated Books of the Year in 2000.

Victor Shade Fairborne in *Rumplestiltskin*

BARRY MOSER is an artist with works on display all over the world. In addition to being an illustrator, he is a printer, painter, print-maker, designer, author, essayist, and teacher. He has illustrated or designed more than 250 books, including *The Divine Comedy of Dante*; Lewis Carroll's *Alice's Adventures in Wonderland*, which won the National Book Award for design and illustration; Joel Chandler Harris and Van Dyke Parks's *Jump Again! The Further Adventures of Brer Rabbit*, which was one of the *New York Times* Ten Best Illustrated Books of the Year; and a collaboration with Cynthia Rylant, *Appalachia: The Voices of Sleeping Birds*, which won the *Boston Globe–Horn Book* Award.

Giselle in *Rumplestiltskin*

MICHAEL PARASKEVAS and his mother, Betty, are the creators and executive producers of three animated series (so far . . . with more on the way): *Maggie and the Ferocious Beast, Marvin the Tap Dancing Horse,* and *The Kids from Room 402.* They have published fourteen children's books, including *Gracie Graves and the Kids from Room 402, The Tangerine Bear,* and *On the Edge of the Sea.* Michael has illustrated for many major magazines, including *Sports Illustrated, Time,* and *Town and Country.* He has an ever-growing toy collection and is a fanatic fan of *The Larry Sanders Show*.

Alberta Louise Johnson in *Little Red Riding Hood*

JERRY PINKNEY has been illustrating children's books since 1964 and has received four Caldecott Honor Medals and four Coretta Scott King Awards. He has been a United States nominee for the Hans Christian Andersen Illustration Medal and has been awarded four gold medals, four silver medals, and the Hamilton King Award from the Society of Illustrators in New York. Pinkney has exhibited his artwork all over the world and has created paintings for the NASA Art Collection at the John F. Kennedy Space Center.

MYLES C. PINKNEY

Goldilocks in *Goldilocks and the Three Bears*

GISELLE POTTER drew a lot as a child because that is what everyone around her did. She and her sister grew up traveling around the world with her parents' puppet theater company. After spending time in Indonesia, she decided to go to art school. Potter's first illustration job was a drawing for the *New Yorker*. Soon after, Chronicle Books published her first book, *Lucy's Eyes and Margaret's Dragon: Lives of the Virgin Saints*. She has since illustrated *The Big Box* by Toni Morrison, *Kate and the Beanstalk* by Mary Pope Osborne, and many other books.

Cosentina Molly "Mama" Bear in *Goldilocks and the Three Bears*

CHRIS RASCHKA is an illustrator, a freelance artist, and a viola player. His book *Yo! Yes?* received a Caldecott Honor Medal in 1994 and was the winner of the UNICEF–Ezra Jack Keats National Award for Children's Book Illustration. Some of his other works include *Charlie Parker Played Be Bop* and *Elizabeth Imagined an Iceberg*.

Prince Blomqvist von Saunabaden in *The Frog Prince*

J. OTTO SEIBOLD's work has appeared in numerous magazines throughout the world and his animation has been featured on MTV and Fox. He is the creator, with his wife Vivian Walsh, of children's books including *Monkey Business, Mr. Lunch Takes a Plane Ride,* and *Olive, the Other Reindeer*, which became an Emmy-nominated television show. His work can also be enjoyed on the Internet at his web site www.jotto.com.

RICHARD TRIMORCHI

Owen "Baby" Bear in *Goldilocks and the Three Bears*

DAVID SHANNON began his career as a freelance editorial illustrator for publications such as the *New York Times, Time* magazine and *Rolling Stone*. Searching for a more mature audience, he began writing and illustrating children's books in 1989, including *How Georgie Radbourn Saved Baseball*, by Larry Johnson, *A Bad Case of Stripes*, and the semi-autobiographical *No, David!* which received a Caldecott Honor Medal in 1999.

Ted E. "Papa" Bear in *Goldilocks and the Three Bears*

CHRIS VAN ALLSBURG studied sculpture in college and exhibited his work in New England and New York City after graduating from the Rhode Island School of Design. In 1979 he wrote and illustrated *The Garden of Abdul Gasazi*, which received a Caldecott Honor Medal. Since then, he has written and illustrated eleven other books, including the Caldecott Medal winners *Jumanji* and *The Polar Express*. He lives in Providence with his wife, Lisa, and daughters, Sophia and Anna.

SCOTT GODWIN PHOTOGRAPHY

ERIC ANTONIOU

The Princess's Pillow in *The Frog Prince*

CYNTHIA VON BUHLER resides in and paints at her castle in Boston. Her work has appeared in hundreds of magazines, and on album covers, novels, and numerous young-adult book covers. She illustrated the picture book *Little Girl in a Red Dress with Cat and Dog* by Nicholas Nicholson. Her paintings have been shown at museums and in galleries across the country, and she has received numerous awards from American Illustration, the Society of Illustrators, and Communication Arts.

The text type was set in Perpetua.

The display type was set in Graymantle and Cafe Mimi.

Color separations by Bright Art (H.K.) Ltd.

Printed and bound by RRDonnelly & Sons, Reynosa, Mexico

This book was printed on Nymolla Matte Art paper.

Production supervision by Kati Banyai

Art direction and design by Denise Cronin

Stories edited by Karen Kushell

STARBRIGHT®

Providing a community where children and teens with illness can connect with peers

STARBRIGHT World™ is a private online network connecting seriously ill children in their homes and in over 95 hospitals across the U.S. and Canada. STARBRIGHT World offers activities designed to promote peer communication and self-expression, enhance feelings of social support, and provide knowledge about illnesses and procedures.

Empowering children with knowledge about medical conditions and procedures

The **STARBRIGHT Explorer Series**™ is a collection of interactive multimedia programs in which children learn about medical conditions and procedures. The series includes programs on Blood Tests, IVs, Medical Imaging, Bone Marrow Aspiration, Spinal Tap, Cystic Fibrosis, Sickle Cell Disease, and Kidney Disease.

Providing peer perspective for teens coping with serious medical conditions

In **STARBRIGHT Videos with Attitude**™, teens talk openly about the challenges they face and their strategies for coping. The series currently includes videos focused on school re-entry, communicating with doctors, and being in the hospital environment.

Easing the anxiety of preschool children undergoing radiation therapy

STARBRIGHT Hospital Pals™ is a tool for healthcare professionals designed to reduce the anxiety and the need for anesthesia in preschool children undergoing radiation therapy for cancer. During treatment, the familiar children's character Barney® narrates stories to the child, providing distraction and companionship.

Motivating children to manage their diabetes

The **STARBRIGHT Diabetes CD-ROM** is a fun-filled interactive adventure that offers children the opportunity to learn and practice diabetes management in an entertaining and engaging manner. Children earn points by keeping simulated blood glucose levels in the normal range.

Educating children about asthma

Coming in 2002 . . . the **STARBRIGHT Asthma CD-ROM** game challenges children to improve their daily asthma management skills. The game combines an engaging storyline and state-of-the-art 3-D animation to teach key concepts in order to help motivate children to practice good decision-making skills.

For further information about STARBRIGHT's programs or research, please visit our Web site at www.starbright.org or call us at 1-800-315-2580
THE STARBRIGHT FOUNDATION 11835 W. Olympic Blvd., Suite 500, Los Angeles, California 90064